Before reading

Look at the book cover toge[...]
Ask, "What do you think will [...]

Turn to the **Key Words** on pa[...]
the child. Draw their attention to the shape of the letters, noting
the tall letters and those that have a tail.

During reading

Offer plenty of support and praise as the child reads the story.
Listen carefully and respond to events in the text.

When a **Key Word** is used for the first time, it is also shown at
the bottom of the page. If the child hesitates over a word, point
to the **New Key Words** box and practise reading it together.
If the word is phonically decodable, you can sound out the
letters and blend the sounds to read the word ("d-o-g, dog").
Praise the child for their effort, then return to the story.

Pause every few pages and ask questions to check the child's
understanding of what they have read. If they begin to lose
concentration, stop reading and save the page for later.

Celebrate the child's achievement and come back to the
story the next day.

After reading

After reading this book, ask, "Did you enjoy the story? What did
you like about it?" Encourage the child to share their opinions.

Use the comprehension questions on page 54 to check the
child's understanding and recall of the text.

Ladybird

Series Consultant: Professor David Waugh
With thanks to Kulwinder Maude

LADYBIRD BOOKS

UK | USA | Canada | Ireland | Australia
India | New Zealand | South Africa

Ladybird Books is part of the Penguin Random House group of companies
whose addresses can be found at global.penguinrandomhouse.com.
www.penguin.co.uk   www.puffin.co.uk   www.ladybird.co.uk

Penguin Random House UK

Original edition of Key Words with Peter and Jane first published by Ladybird Books Ltd 1964
Series updated 2023
This book first published 2023
001

With thanks to Liz Pemberton for her contributions in advising on the illustrations
With thanks to Inclusive Minds for connecting us with their Inclusion Ambassador network,
and in particular thanks to Guntaas Kaur Chugh for her input on the illustrations

Printed in China

The authorized representative in the EEA is Penguin Random House Ireland,
Morrison Chambers, 32 Nassau Street, Dublin D02 YH68

A CIP catalogue record for this book is available from the British Library

ISBN: 978-0-241-51100-8

All correspondence to:
Ladybird Books
Penguin Random House Children's
One Embassy Gardens, 8 Viaduct Gardens, London SW11 7BW

Key Words

with Peter and Jane

10a

Let's go camping!

Based on the original
Key Words with Peter and Jane
reading scheme and research by William Murray

Original edition written by William Murray
This edition written by Ben Hulme-Cross
Illustrated by Pablo Gallego with colour work by János Orban
Based on characters and design by Gustavo Mazali

afternoon began breakfast

by computer different

doctor even family film

fire got great happy

kitchen laugh lots love

morning much music

online or people right

room snow still stop

table television then these

those thought told town

 breakfast

 computer

 doctor

 family

 film

 fire

 kitchen

 music

 people

 room

 snow

 table

 television

 town

One morning at breakfast, Peter and Jane were sitting at the kitchen table. Mum was on the computer.

"Are we going this morning?" asked Peter.

"Going where?" Mum asked.

"Camping!" Peter and Jane yelled. They were very happy about the trip.

Tess barked. She was happy too.

New Key Words

| morning | breakfast | kitchen |
| table | computer | happy |

"I love it that you're so happy!" Mum said. "We're going this afternoon. Look at this. There are lots of pictures online of where we're camping."

Mum turned the computer round. There really were lots of pictures online. There were happy people and a dog playing in the snow.

"They all look so happy! Will it snow this afternoon?" said Peter.

"No, it won't snow," Mum said to him.

New Key Words

love	afternoon	lots	online
	people	snow	

"Do we have to wait until this afternoon to go?" Jane asked.

"We'll see. We have so much to pack!" Mum said. "Can you put away the breakfast things and clear the kitchen table? Then, I'll put a film on in the living room for you."

Peter and Jane got up from the kitchen table and put the breakfast things away. Then, they saw a film in the other room.

In the afternoon, they all got into the car. There wasn't much room because there were lots of camping things.

Dad put on some music. They had music on all afternoon as they passed town after town after town.

When the car stopped, the camp looked even better than the pictures online. Even Tess was happy!

New Key Words

music   town   stop   even

"I love this place!" said Dad. "It's not like being in town. No televisions. No films. No computers."

"Dad's happy!" said Jane with a laugh. "No televisions. No films. No computers. But I can hear some music. Can we go and play?"

"Yes, those children by that van are having lots of fun," Mum told them. "Why not play with them?"

The children were called Adam and Mia.

"Come and see our van," said Mia. "We've even taken it camping in the snow before!"

New Key Words

television   laugh   those   by   told

Mia and Adam's dad was working on his computer. There was even a television in the van.

"You've got so much room!" Peter said. "And lots of things. Our dad says no televisions or films or computers on this trip."

"Your dad's right," Mia's dad told them. "We're not in town now. I have my computer for work, but Mia and Adam will not see many films or much television when we are here."

"My dad's a doctor," Mia told Peter and Jane. "He's called Doctor Sharp."

New Key Words

or   right   doctor

Mum and Dad had put the family
tent up, and there was a campfire by
the table.

"I love your dog!" Adam told the family.
"I told my dad that I want a dog."

"She's called Tess," Peter told him.
"Come and say hello."

"Yes, come in," Jane said. "We don't
have a kitchen or a television or films,
but it's still great!"

"I'd love to have a television and a computer in the tent," Peter told Adam.

"You know what I think about that," called Dad from the campfire.

"No television. No films. No computers!" said Peter and Jane, and they all laughed.

Peter showed Adam his comic book. "I love comics so much," he said. "This one's about some people stopping a snow monster from taking over their town!"

Jane showed Mia her new hat.

"Those pom-poms look like snowballs," said Mia.

New Key Words

"Let's meet by the van after dinner,"
Mia said. "We can play hide-and-seek.
It'll be great!"

Peter and Jane sat down at the table
by the fire.

"It's great you've met those children,"
said Mum.

"Their dad's a doctor," said Peter.

"And their van's great," Jane told them.
"There's so much room, and there's a
kitchen."

"It's even got a television to see films on,"
said Peter.

Dad laughed and said, "We have all
the room we could want out here!"

New Key Words

After dinner, Mum and Dad stayed by the fire.

Peter and Jane found Mia and Adam sitting at their kitchen table.

"Dad, we're going to play," said Mia. "We want lots and lots of time to have lots and lots of fun!"

"Right, you've got until . . ." Doctor Sharp thought for a bit. "There's still some daylight, so you can stop playing when it's dark."

"Great! We've got lots of time for hide-and-seek then!" said Adam.

New Key Words

thought

Peter began to count down. "Ten . . . nine . . ." he said.

"That's not much time," said Jane, running away with Mia.

"There's a big tree with lots of room to hide!" said Mia.

Sitting on different branches, they could see all the people down by the campfires. Some people were singing by their fires.

"I love music," said Mia with a happy laugh, "and all these fires look great."

"Look, there's Adam!" said Mia. Adam had stopped by Peter and Jane's family tent.

Adam said something to Peter and Jane's mum and dad, then he walked into their tent.

"Some people still aren't very good at this game, even if they play it all the time!" said Mia, laughing. "That's not a great hiding place. Adam should have thought of somewhere different!"

New Key Words

Peter began to look for the others. First, he stopped at Doctor Sharp's van.

Then, Peter thought he would go to the family tent. Mum and Dad were still sitting at the table by the fire.

"Have you seen Mia or Adam, those new friends of ours?" Peter asked. "Or Jane?"

"Stop! Stop! You shouldn't even ask," Dad said, laughing. "We can't tell you."

"Right," said Peter. "I'll look in a different place."

New Key Words

Mia and Jane saw Adam crawl out of the family tent and run to the van. Then, they heard a happy laugh.

"Got you!" Peter said, looking right up at them. "Those branches are a great place to hide! I thought you'd still be by the tent or by the van. Is Adam somewhere different?"

"Right, I'll give you a hint," Mia said. "He's somewhere to the right of that green tent, where those people are playing music."

New Key Words

Doctor Sharp was still working on his computer at the kitchen table.

"I didn't trick you," Doctor Sharp began, looking up at Peter from his computer and laughing. "Adam wasn't here before."

Adam was happy that he was the winner. He told Peter how he had hidden in Peter's family tent first, and then in the van. Peter thought that was great.

"I found Jane and Mia in the big tree," Peter told him.

New Key Words

When the boys got to the family tent, Mum and Dad were still by the fire. The girls were in the tent.

"My new hat's missing!" Jane said. "So is your comic, Peter."

"Let's think of all the different places they could be," said Adam. "Then, we'll look there."

"Look for what?" Dad asked. "You're not looking online, are you? I told you, the best thing about being away from town is no television and no computer!"

New Key Words

"No, Dad, we're not looking online," said Jane. "I can't find my hat. I got it out to show Mia just this afternoon."

"Right!" said Mia. "Where have we been playing? Let's look in all those places. Jane, we'll look in the van. The boys can keep looking here."

Peter and Adam looked in the family tent. Then, they began looking by the table and by the fire.

When Jane and Mia got to the van, Doctor Sharp was sitting at the table.

"Still playing?" he asked. "Or have you stopped?"

They told Doctor Sharp why they were there. He turned off the computer and helped them look, but they couldn't find the comic or the hat.

"Do you think Adam and Peter could have found them in our family tent or by the fire?" asked Jane.

"I don't know," said Mia. "Let's look by the tree."

New Key Words

Jane and Mia looked by the tree trunk. Then, they walked back to the tent.

"No luck?" Peter asked.

"Not much," said Mia.

"We'd better go over to our van," Adam said to Mia. "It's getting dark now."

"Sit down by the fire," said Mum to Peter and Jane. "Maybe we'll find your hat and comic in the morning."

New Key Words

Peter and Jane were still unhappy in the morning. They got dressed, and Dad put breakfast on the table. Then, Tess got up and stretched.

"Jane!" said Peter. "Look at Tess's bed!"

There were Jane's hat and Peter's comic.

"Tess! We were looking for these!" said Jane, laughing.

"I told you we'd find them in the morning," said Mum.

New Key Words

They walked over to the breakfast table and told Dad.

"Adam and Mia will laugh when we tell them," said Peter.

Peter and Jane had their breakfast at the table. Then, they got the hat and the comic and walked with Tess to Mia and Adam's van.

"Look at all these tents," said Jane as they walked. "It's like a little town!"

"Even more people might come this afternoon," said Peter. "Then it will look even more like a town."

New Key Words

Doctor Sharp was sitting by the door of the van.

"Good morning!" he said.

Adam and Mia were eating breakfast. They saw the hat and the comic.

"You found them! That's great!" said Mia.

"It was Tess," Peter said. "They were in her bed! No one thought of looking there."

Tess trotted up to Mia and Adam and began licking them and wagging her tail.

Adam began to laugh. Soon, Mia was laughing too. Then, they were all laughing! Tess began jumping and barking happily.

They all wanted to play a game.

"Hide-and-seek?" asked Jane.

"I know an even better one," Adam told them. "It's called 'Hide the hat'!"

New Key Words

Questions

Answer these questions about the story.

1 Who do Peter and Jane meet at the camp?

2 What game do all the children play after dinner?

3 In the game, where do Jane and Mia hide?

4 How do you think Peter and Jane feel when they see that their comic and hat are missing?

5 Where do the children find the missing comic and hat?

6 What game does Adam say they should play the next morning?